Ninja Pug 2

The Truth Revealed

Amma Lee

INTRODUCTION

Jiro and Luna are back in "The Truth Revealed" and this time the two ninja dogs are uncovering secrets that never in their wildest dreams they thought would ever happen. Not only are they still tracking down the ninjas who had stolen books from Jiro's owner and friend Hanzo, but now they must stop the ninja organization's evil plan regarding the president. Things are moving fast for our ninja dog heroes, but Jiro's determination to figure out the truth will ultimately prevail. In the second installment of the Ninja Dogs series, readers follow Jiro and Luna on their journey towards the truth, and the truth regarding the mysterious ninja boy Ryo, Hanzo, Monukuma, and Luna will have readers shocked and on the edge of their seats wanting more!

CHAPTER ONE

Jiro could feel himself breathing heavily as he chased after the dark silhouette. He was a dog, so he should have been faster than the human. Every time Jiro thought he was closing in some of the distance between him and the assailant, the human widened the gap between them.

"Tsk! Come back here!" Jiro screamed, but it was in vain. The dark figure disappeared in a cloud of white smoke. Stopping, Jiro growled angrily. He needed to catch the boy because there were so many things that he wanted to ask him. Why was he doing this? Why is he stealing from Hanzo? And the most important question, who is he?

Jiro looked around the forest as he sniffed, trying to find any signs of humans being there. He could not. "How could I let him get away?!" Jiro shouted out angrily. The boy had stolen some books from Hanzo that could apparently help the thieving ninjas learn some powerful new techniques. Techniques powerful enough to do real damage to the world. Jiro had to get the books back because he knew that they were in the hands of the enemy.

"Humph! Looks like you're too stupid to be a real ninja," Jiro quickly snapped his head back and saw the figure that he was chasing behind him. When did he get there and why couldn't Jiro sense him? *It's too late though*, Jiro thought, as the dark figure quickly placed a bag over his head.

"No!" Jiro woke up from his nightmare. He was breathing heavily as he looked around. Instead of seeing a dark forest, Jiro saw the kitchen. Had he fallen asleep while eating his food? "Then... that was a dream?" Jiro asked himself. It had been a few weeks since ninjas had broken into his and Hanzo's home to steal some valuable books. It had also been weeks since Luna, the white poodle, and Jiro had infiltrated the ninjas' headquarters and engaged in battle. Ever since that day, Jiro has dreamt about one of the ninjas that they'd encountered.

Jiro stood up and shook out his short fur. The little pug normally didn't have nightmares. Those were things that humans were subjected to, but recently nightmares have became an ongoing thing for him. He felt uneasy, and he knew he needed to go take a walk. Looking outside and listening to Hanzo snoring in the next room, Jiro knew that it was late, well after midnight.

"I won't be long," Jiro said. Hanzo didn't want him going out too often at night, especially when Hanzo wasn't there with him, but Jiro had to disobey his friend's rule. He needed to go outside because staying inside wouldn't help him clear his thoughts. Walking outside into the night's cold air, Jiro inhaled and exhaled slowly.

"A little late for a dog like you to be out here," Jiro heard a voice speaking to him. "An owl might swoop down and get you!" There was no way possible for Jiro not to know that voice. It was the voice of the white poodle, Luna.

"I can say the same thing about you," was Jiro's response. Jiro looked towards the house next door to see Luna lying on the ground with her white fur basking in the moonlight. Jiro wondered if Luna always came outside after dark alone. "Bored?" Jiro asked.

"No... I couldn't sleep," Luna said honestly. *I see, so Luna has a lot on her mind as well*, Jiro thought. Jiro walked over to the part of the gate that had plenty of wear and tear and burrowed his way under to the other side. Soon, Jiro was standing by Luna's side. Luna didn't mind his presence though. Even though this was the only time that she had to be alone and think, she didn't mind Jiro joining her.

"I had a nightmare," Jiro said, starting up a conversation. "That I was in the forest chasing after that ninja from before. I believe the humans referred to him as Ryo," Luna listened to Jiro talking, making sure not to interrupt him. It was very rare that Jiro spoke to her. Jiro had asked her a lot of questions after working together to find the thieves that broke into his and Hanzo's house, but Jiro had gotten mad at Luna for not answering his questions and hadn't spoken to her in a while. Luna was glad that they were back on speaking terms.

"You have a lot on your mind, huh? You really think that boy is the old man's grandson?" Luna asked. It was starting to drizzle, and if her fur got wet, her owner would know what she's been up to.

"I'm not 100% confident, but something is telling me

that he is. If not, he has at the very least been in contact with Hanzo's grandson," Jiro stopped talking then as Luna made her way back onto her porch getting ready to go in the house. "Luna... I'm going to hunt for him and the rest of the ninjas down starting tomorrow. They're planning something evil, and I have to stop them."

"Good luck," Luna said, and Jiro sighed irritably.

"I need your help!" Jiro barked. "But first, please... I want you to tell me the truth about who you really are." Luna knew that this was going to come up again and since she knew that she could be a great help to Jiro, she finally decided to tell him.

****

"What's the plan, Jiro?" Luna asked, as Jiro paced back and forth in the basement of his and Hanzo's house. After the old man's training, Hanzo told Jiro that he had some business to take care of and that he'd be back later. Jiro thought it would be a good idea for Luna and Jiro to train together considering what he had just learned about the sarcastic poodle. Luna came from a long line of ninja dogs of the Tosa Clan! Never in Jiro's wildest dreams did he ever believe that dogs, other than him, were capable of being ninjas.

"We need to go back to the ninjas' hideout and follow their scent from there." Even though Jiro got back the photo that Hanzo was mainly sad about losing, Jiro still had unfinished business. Whatever the ninjas were planning, he needed to stop it. Also, if that boy was really Hanzo's grandson, Jiro had to do everything in his power to save him.

"What happens if we're not able to follow their scent?" Luna asked. It's been weeks since they've left. Jiro and Luna might have been dogs, but they weren't exactly young pups anymore.

"We'll find it, Luna. We're not pups any longer, but we've got the determination to make things happen! Please don't sell us short!" Especially after learning that Luna was a ninja, there was no way that they would fail.

"Well… let me think about it. I don't want to make any decisions right now since it's so late." Luna bowed and went through the doggy door to her house. "Let's talk tomorrow when the sun's out. I should know for sure by then."

"Of course," Jiro didn't want Luna to feel pressured to decide, but that didn't mean that he wanted her to exercise her right to tell him no. He needed Luna's help. Without Luna's help, Jiro was sure that he wouldn't be able to pull it off himself. "Sleep well. I'll see you tomorrow." Jiro turned around then just as it was beginning to start pouring down.

Once Jiro was in the house, he stopped to listen to his surroundings. *Good, Hanzo's still sleeping.* Jiro believed that if he was to go to bed now that he'd only have another bad dream. Jiro wasn't really in the mood to go to sleep anyways. Shaking out his wet fur, Jiro made his way downstairs to train. If he was going to take down some ninjas, he needed to get into top notch shape. It wasn't going to be easy taking on human opponents, but he knew it wouldn't be impossible either.

"I need to figure out what evil they're planning and find a way to stop their plans. I also need to know for sure if that Ryo boy is Hanzo's grandson." Having to stop an evil plan from unfurling and possibly rescuing someone was not going to be an easy task. Standing in front of Hanzo's worn down punching bag, Jiro stood on his two back paws, jumped, and did a spinning backflip kick, and knocked the punching bag over. He was pleased with being able to do that, but he knew it wasn't going to be enough.

Jiro was going to work hard for the rest of the night, wake Hanzo up so that he could practice, and then Jiro will practice again as soon as Hanzo was busy.

"It's going to be a long night," Jiro mumbled, as he continued to attack the punching bag with everything that he had.

CHAPTER TWO

Jiro's every day routine was to wake Hanzo up at 5 am for his martial arts training. Since Hanzo came from a family of powerful ninjas, despite his old age, he still trained his body. After Hanzo had trained for a few hours, washed up, and prepared both him and Jiro something to eat, he frequently took a short nap. Recently, however; Hanzo has been leaving in the mornings and coming home at night. This started happening after the robbery, and Jiro was surprised that Hanzo hasn't said anything about where he goes every day.

"Earth to Jiro," Jiro shook his head clearing his thoughts when he heard Luna's voice. She was staring at him with wide eyes. Jiro remembered that Luna watched his every move, so he needed to tell himself to stop spacing out all the time.

"Sorry, what were you saying?" Jiro asked, as Luna came over to him and sat down. They were in the basement of Jiro's home training, but it was time for them to start thinking about leaving. Jiro was nervous, but this was something that needed to be done. Luna sighed.

"I didn't agree to help you out to watch you look on in a daze, Jiro," Luna said irritably. Though Luna had a fun and somewhat sarcastic nature, she didn't have a problem telling it like it is. "Are we leaving or not? Unlike your owner, mine often looks for me during the day. We need to take this show on the road!"

"Right, sorry I just have a lot on my mind," Jiro said, and Luna nodded her head in agreement. The pug certainly did have a lot on his mind. Luna was aware that Jiro was stressed out, but being stressed wasn't going to help them in their mission. If Jiro wanted to get back the missing books, uncover the ninjas' ultimate plan, and find out if that kid was Hanzo's grandson, then Jiro needed to be alert and not overly-emotional.

"So, are we going to finish training or are we going to head out? It's not going to be daytime forever." Luna said, and Jiro nodded his head.

"Let's head out now. The earlier the better, right? It might take a few hours to track their location, but I'm confident with yours and my combined knowledge that we will be successful." Jiro was confident in their abilities, but he sincerely hoped that it'd be enough. If a battle did take place, it'd be incredibly difficult to take on all the ninjas at the same time. So, if it did happen that way, Jiro wanted to at the very least make sure that his head was clear.

Jiro and Luna made their way out of the house and followed the same trail that they had followed weeks prior. It didn't take them long to make it to the ninjas' former hideout, and from the looks and smell of things, the ninjas had never come back.

"Well…. what are you waiting for?" Luna asked. "Let's walk around the building and see if we can pick up their scent." Jiro thought that was a logical idea, but Jiro thought about something else they should do before going to look for them. Jiro was sure that it wouldn't take too long.

"Wait," Jiro said and Luna turned towards him. "Let's check in the building first. They might have left clues to where they're going and what they're planning." Luna smiled after Jiro had said that. Now, Jiro was indeed beginning to see the big picture.

"Lead the way," Luna said, and Jiro grinned showing his little sharp canine teeth. They made their way through the abandoned hideout, occasionally stopping to review some of the paperwork that was thrown around. Though they were dogs, they both had the ability to read. "These look like some type of blueprints," Luna said, as she came across some paperwork with a drawing of a building.

"Let me look at it," Jiro said as he made his way to Luna. Peering over her shoulder, Jiro saw a picture of a building with various entry points and comments on who would enter in and where. Jiro wasn't entirely sure, but he felt that this was not a new facility that was in the process of being created. Jiro had the suspicious feeling that he had seen this building before.

"What do you think these are blueprints for?" Luna asked. She, like Jiro, had a feeling that she's seen this building before. She felt it in the pit of her stomach, and it was making her nervous. Luna could feel in her heart, that this was an important place and that these ninjas should not have the blueprints for this location.

"This is…the blueprint is…" Jiro repeatedly said as he searched the deepest part of his brain. The building is a grand and important place. A building that is usually occupied by humans in the secret services and FBI, but it was a vacation home to someone important. It was on the tip of Jiro's tongue. Just then, the answer appeared in Jiro's mind, and the look on Jiro's face was priceless. If Luna had to describe Jiro's expression, it was as if his favorite chew toy was run over by a hundred cars.

"Jiro, what's wrong?" Luna asked in concern when Jiro didn't say anything.

"The President!!!!" Jiro shouted. Even with such a vague response, Luna understood fully what the blueprint was.

The blueprint was for the president's vacation home.

****

"We must hurry!" Jiro said as he and Luna bolted out of the hideout and made their way downtown. Jiro wasn't entirely sure of what story those blueprints told, but he was confident that the ninjas meant to do something terrible to the president. Why else would they have a blueprint for every possible way to enter the historic building with details describing areas that were safer to enter?

"Do you think they plan to kidnap the president?" Luna asked as they ducked and dodged through the crowd of people who were out and about on the street.

"I don't know, but whatever they're planning it doesn't

look good." If the boy that Jiro fought was Ryoichi, why was he going along with whatever those ninjas are planning? What happened to him after the accident? Was he kidnapped? Is he rebelling because of what happened to his father? Whatever the case may be, Jiro still did not know if Ryo and Ryoichiwere one and the same.

"What's the plan? We can't just walk in there and tell the president that he's in trouble. One, he wouldn't be able to understand us. Two, I doubt his bodyguards are going to let two running dogs get near the president, and I'm not fond of being tranquilized." Jiro growled then. Not at Luna, but at the situation at hand. He knew full well that warning the president wasn't going to be an easy feat. However, no matter what, they were going to save him.

"I haven't thought that far ahead yet," Jiro answered honestly. Jiro was never one to adequately prepare and plan for an attack. He was a "do it as you go" type of dog. "But at any rate, if we're not too late, I know we will be victorious!" Jiro said confidently. No one could ever say that Jiro was not determined. When he set his mind on doing something, Jiro followed through till the very end. That was a trait that he got from the determined Hanzo.

"Oh boy," Luna said with a slight chuckle. "What are we going to do about you? You're always running head first into danger." Any other dog, Luna would have thought they were a complete moron if they did the same things that Jiro did. However, she could not find it in her heart to think the same about Jiro. Luna knew that when it came to something important, Jiro would be able to do anything, especially with Luna by his side.

After almost an hour of running, Jiro and Luna had made

it to their destination. They were relieved to see the place in one piece, but there was a familiar confusing scent that lingered through the air. Jiro and Luna looked at each other both recognizing that smell. It was the ninjas, they were somewhere close.

CHAPTER THREE

Jiro and Luna looked around as they sniffed the ground around them. They had learned a few weeks ago that the ninjas who worked out the plan to break into Hanzo's and Jiro's house had the ability to hide their scent. Since Jiro and Luna were dogs, it didn't work on them completely, but the ninjas' abilities did try to fool their sense of smell.

"I think they're in this building," Luna said as she moved closer to a building with the words "Hotel Maria" on the side of the building. Jiro and Luna weren't sure what exactly a hotel was, but they did understand that it wasn't a permanent residence for humans, just a temporary stay. Jiro and Hanzo stayed at a hotel for one summer before when they were on "vacation." Jiro didn't understand what a hotel or a vacation was, but when they went back home a few days later, Jiro knew it was only an occasional temporary thing.

"Let's climb up that tree and look through the window. It looks pretty dark in there, which is rather odd," Jiro said as he jumped onto a small ledge and pushed off his paws to plant his nails firmly into the tree. "These types of places are always lit up," Jiro said, and Luna followed behind him and climbed up the tree.

"This isn't one of those things dogs should be doing," Luna said as she shifted awkwardly on the tree branch that they were sitting on to get a closer look in the nearest window. Luna had chased plenty of cats up a tree, but not ever once had she climbed up a tree after them.

"Shh... ninjas have the ability to do anything. It doesn't matter if this isn't something Jiro and Luna the dog would do. Jiro and Luna, the ninja, will do it," Jiro said as his small eyes peered through the window. It was dark in the hotel and Jiro couldn't understand why. Did the electricity get cut off or something of that nature?

Jiro looked around the dark room to see if he saw any movement, but after a while, Jiro figured they'd need to check on the higher floors as well. As Jiro was about to climb further up the tree, Luna stopped him.

"Wait, I can hear movement now," Luna said, and Jiro turned his attention back to the window. He cleared his mind and only focused on hearing possible sounds. It didn't take Jiro long to hear footsteps and two deep voices.

"Monukuma-sensei, how should we proceed in getting rid of the president's bodyguards?" Jiro and Luna gasped. Jiro and Luna remembered that name well as they got acquainted with the leader of the ninjas who they encountered a few weeks ago.

"We have to continue watching their every movement," Monukuma said. "We can have some of our students handle them one by one. It shouldn't be too hard because we've got some pretty good gems in our clan."

"Did they take over this hotel?" Jiro asked himself. This had to be the case because why else would this always busy hotel be so dark in the middle of the day.

"So, they *are* planning on doing something to the president," Luna said. Jiro had mentioned that the president was probably in trouble because of the blueprints they found at the ninjas' former hideout. The fact that Monukuma spoke about getting rid of the president's bodyguards practically confirmed it.

"Ootori, get a few of our promising ninjas to scope out the place. I need to know exactly how many people are on staff."

"Sir!" In a blink of an eye, Ootori was gone.

"Soon everything will be in place. Everything will go as planned." Monukuma let out a boisterous laugh and disappeared. Jiro and Luna looked at each other with apparent worry in their eyes. What they had just heard, did not sound good.

****

"You sure this is going to work?" Luna asked, as they made their way down the chimney. Jiro wasn't knowledgeable with technology and didn't have any fancy equipment, so his plan to bypass through all the hotel's security measures was to infiltrate the building via the chimney.

"Of course, Luna. Have some faith in us," Jiro said as he slowly made his way down the narrow chimney. It was difficult because Jiro's sharp nails often made him slide with each step that he took.

"It's not that I don't have faith in us, it's just that this plan…. it's not one of your smarter ideas," Luna said honestly. Luna wasn't against being blunt, but she didn't want to anger the small pug when they were climbing down a chimney. What would happen to them if they fell all the way down it? "To be completely honest, this plan is absurd. What if someone lights a fire?"

"Humans have unique natures about themselves, but it's 90 degrees outside, Luna. Only a fool would want to make the place hotter." Jiro caught himself from falling after his paws slipped for the hundredth time in the past five minutes." Luna was uncomfortable, and at that moment she was starting to think that Jiro had lost his mind.

"It's not too late to find another way in," Luna said again. Luna didn't like fire, so the thought of someone possibly lighting the fireplace didn't sit well with the poodle.

"Relax Luna," Jiro reassured her again. "This part will be over soon. The quicker we get in and put a stop to these ninjas' evil plan, the quicker we can forget that this ever happened." Jiro also wanted to find out more about Ryo, but he didn't mention that part to Luna. After a few more minutes of climbing down the chimney, they finally made it to the bottom.

The room they had entered had the blinds closed. Poking their heads out from the small opening of the fireplace, they sighed a sigh of relief when they saw that there wasn't anyone in the room.
"Okay, Luna," Jiro started. "We need to get in here and

stop whatever it is that these people are doing. We might have to go into battle to accomplish this goal. While we're here, we also need to keep our eyes opened for the books. We can't let them hurt the president, and we can't let them use Hanzo's books for evil." Jiro spoke quickly, and he was slightly out of breath when he had finished talking. He was nervous, but if they remained optimistic, they should be okay.

"That's it? No explanation on how we're going to get these details done?" Luna was still feeling a little anxious from before, but her anxiety was slowly going away.

"No… we go in, and we get things done by any means necessary!" Jiro said confidently with a smile on his furry face. Luna didn't think that this was the time to be smiling happily like this, but Jiro's smile was contagious, and she found herself smiling at the little pug.

"Alright boss, lead the way," Luna said. Jiro nodded his head, thankful that Luna decided to trust him. They were going to be victorious because Jiro and Luna were a team. Jiro hated to admit this, but he couldn't see himself being there in that situation with any dog other than Luna. He would have never thought that a few weeks ago.

"Luna, let's do this!" Jiro said enthusiastically.

CHAPTER FOUR

Jiro and Luna kept a low profile as they made their way through the large hotel. Several ninjas and ninjas in training roamed the halls, but the stealthy ninja dogs made sure to not be seen. Both Jiro and Luna were nervous, but for the most part, they were confident in their skills.

"So, what do you think we're going to do with the president?" Jiro recognized the boy's voice that had spoken. When Jiro looked up, it was Ryo.

"I don't know," said a ninja that neither Jiro nor Luna had ever seen before. "I hear Monukuma-sensei has the ability to brainwash people. Maybe he's planning on influencing the president too for our purposes."

"Brainwash?" Jiro whispered and cleared everything from his mind. He wanted to make sure that he heard everything that the boys were saying. He also wanted to see if this Ryo boy said or did anything that proved that he's Ryoichi.

"Jiro, we have to move it before we're discovered!" Luna whispered irritably. Though the dogs shield themselves from anyone's vision by walking under long curtains, that didn't mean they were completely out of view from spectators. If a powerful ninja was to show up now, Luna was positive that it wouldn't take them long to notice their presence.

"Just a little longer, they might let something slip," Jiro responded before clearing his mind to take in everything that the young ninjas would say. Luna sighed. Sure, the little runts might let something slip, but Luna doubted that the apparent low-level ninjas would know much. Luna was sure that Jiro was doing this because of that Ryo kid. Luna understood that Jiro was curious about the boy, but that wasn't the time since they were trying to be stealthy.

"I know that you're expecting us to have to battle them," Luna said. "But that doesn't mean to increase the chances of that happening!" Jiro thought about what Luna had just said and sighed. The poodle was right, and he should keep his eye on the main goal of the situation.

"You're right..." Jiro said and continued walking forward.

"Wait a minute," Jiro and Luna froze in place when they heard Ryo's voice. His voice sounded like he was suspicious of something. "Does it feel... odd in here?" Ryo asked the boy next to him. Jiro and Luna heard a body shifting from side to side.

"Now that you mention it... something does feel off."

"Let's look around," Ryo said, and Jiro and Luna could feel their little hearts stop. The ninjas might have been young, but Jiro and Luna underestimated them. They thought they'd be able to sneak past the humans because Jiro and Luna were dogs, but it appears that they can sense beings other than humans.

"When I say run, you better run," Jiro said and Luna nodded her head. She knew sneaking out there was a bad idea. Jiro heard the two ninjas searching around and Jiro had never been this afraid in his life. He was prepared to possibly enter a fight, but the whole experience of this situation was nerve-wrecking.

"Look up," the other boy's voice broke the silence. Ryo did as he was told and chuckled.

"Cameras, I should have known. Let's move on, we're being watched. Sensei might think we're slacking off!" Ryo didn't wait for the other boy to respond. He pulled a small round object out of his pocket and threw it on the ground. White smoke filled the area, and when it dispersed, the two young ninjas were gone.

"Jiro," Luna began when she was sure that the coast was clear. "I understand what you want to do and I am for it, especially if that boy is family. However, that can wait. We need to find the books and stop whatever these people are planning. After that's done, please feel free to investigate that human," Jiro sighed and nodded his head.

"Yes, let's go now. Too much time has already been wasted," Jiro was ashamed that he didn't have his priorities straight. If they had engaged in a fight right now and had been captured, that would have been all his fault. Jiro was grateful that he had Luna there to keep him on his paws. They needed to be careful and not blow their cover so early in the mission. Jiro vowed to himself that he would keep his eyes on the prize.

****

"Everyone in position," Jiro and Luna rounded a corner to see a lot of ninjas looking out of a window in a grand room. The room appeared to be a dining room, but all the tables and chairs were pushed to the back of the room. "We don't have a lot of time; I fear that the police might be on their way as we speak," Monukuma said as he directed his subordinates. To Jiro and Luna, it looked as if they were getting ready to execute their plan. Jiro couldn't let that happen, but he didn't know what he should do.

"What should we do? What should we do?" Jiro asked over and over as he tried to figure out a plan. It was times like this that he wished that he had preplanned things.

"Take down the bodyguards, and you know what to do with the president," Monukuma said. Luna pushed her head into Jiro's side.

"We have to do something quick!" Luna whispered, and Jiro's tail started wagging hard. Things were happening so fast, and Jiro didn't know what to do.

"Hey… looks like that old man is there too," Jiro heard Ryo's voice then.

"That's the owner of the books, and he's walking out with the president!" Another voice said. Jiro's head snapped up at that. *Hanzo! What's he doing with the president?!* Jiro thought. He couldn't let anything happen to the president, but most importantly, he couldn't let anything happen to his dear friend Hanzo.

"I won't let you do anything!" Jiro barked and dashed towards the crowd of ninjas.

"Monukuma-sensei! It's those pesky mutts again!" A ninja screamed from the crowd as he made a dash towards Jiro. Jiro dodged the boy's attack and tripped the boy. Ninjas made their way towards Jiro, but he dodged them and counterattacked them with every move. Luna looked around and saw Jiro taking on each and every ninja as he made his way towards the end of the room. Luna knew what she needed to do. As Jiro progressed through the crowd, Luna made her way further down the stairs to go outside.

"Heh, looks like your partner left you," Monukuma said as Jiro made his way to him. "Smart dog, but you, on the other hand, couldn't be more naïve." Monukuma couldn't speak dog or anything of that nature, but considering the skills that Jiro possessed, he was certain that the dog could understand him well. "I hear you gave my boys some problems last time. No matter, you live and you learn. But you… my little naïve pup will not spoil our plans."

"That's where you're wrong!" Jiro shouted and jumped high in the air. He was preparing to attack Monukuma with everything that he had.

"Fire!" Monukuma shouted. Jiro saw Ryo moving his arms to aim at something and without thinking, Jiro directed all his energy from Monukuma to Ryo. Hanzo's grandson or not, he didn't hold back his power. Ryo's hand was forced down, and the next thing that Jiro heard was the sound of the glass from the window shattering.

He didn't know what had just happened, but he listened to a lot of commotion from outside. There were a lot of people screaming, and Jiro had the nagging suspicion that it had to do with what had just happened.

"Jiro!!" Jiro froze when his name was called. Jiro recognized the voice that called out to him. Jiro had heard this voice every day for many years. Turning around slowly, Jiro's eyes landed on Hanzo.

CHAPTER FIVE

"You," Hanzo said looking past Jiro towards the man behind him.

"You," the deep angry voice of Monukuma responded. Jiro stopped when he saw Luna coming in behind Hanzo. Jiro made a face that if his facial expression was put into words would say, "Did you leave to get Hanzo?"

"I see you've hijacked this hotel for your own selfish and evil ways," Hanzo said walking closer to Monukuma. The young ninjas who Jiro had knocked down were slowly making their way to their feet. They were surprised that they had been bested by a dog... a pug at that!

"Humph... I should have known that you would have been with the president," Monukuma said, and Jiro looked from Hanzo to Monukuma confused. *Why would Hanzo have been with the president?* Jiro thought to himself.

Jiro walked close to Jiro then and patted him on the head.

"You should be at home," Hanzo said in a firm voice. "Imagine my surprise when Luna came out of the hotel. I knew something had to be going on in here, but I wouldn't have imagined that you'd be here."

"Ah... so you know this bothersome pooch?" Monukuma asked with an evil grin on his face. Hanzo frowned.

"It doesn't matter. Like I was saying, when I heard the president was going to be in town and when my Hakumoto books were stolen, I figured that you were planning something like this. It's been years since we've trained together, but I always remembered you saying that you always wanted to be a ruler versus being ruled. I'm old now, but I haven't lost my skill or wit!" Jiro couldn't believe what he was hearing! Hanzo and Monukuma used to train together and even then Monukuma was plotting evil? This was surely many years ago.

"Impressive... only you could put two and two together like that. But sorry, you're too late. The deed's done. The president is down." Hanzo chuckled and walked away from Jiro. Once he was a little bit away from his friend, Hanzo got into a fighting stance. Monukuma let out a bark of laughter and did the same. Jiro knew that Hanzo could fight well for being an old man, but he had never actually seen him in action with another person! Jiro knew that he shouldn't be excited about this, but he was.

"Sorry pal, but you got him in the arm. We have the best medical facilities in the world. The president will be up and at it again in a week or two tops!" It was apparent that Monukuma didn't like what he had just heard. He frowned and yelled so loud that Jiro thought his ears would split. In a blink of an eye, Monukuma lunged his body towards Hanzo. Hanzo was expecting the attack and jumped high into the air and did a front flip so that he landed behind Monukuma.

"Look at him go," Luna whispered to Jiro. The ninjas all had risen, but nobody dared to jump in. Everyone was clearly in awe of the two old mens' abilities. Hanzo dodged Monukuma's attacks with ease, and Monukuma was barely able to catch his breath at how fast Hanzo was.

"Hey… we should help Monukuma-sensei!" Ryo shouted and made his way over to his sensei. Ryo had never encountered anyone who was able to dodge and land a hit on Monukuma before. Others were about to follow Ryo's lead, but police sirens could be heard outside.

"Everyone retreat! Retreat!" Ootori, Monukuma's right-hand man, shouted. In a blink of an eye, everyone was gone but Jiro, Hanzo, Luna, Monukuma, and Ryo.

"Luna! We have to subdue Ryo!" Jiro shouted, and Luna nodded her head. Jiro and Luna made a run towards Ryo.

"Tsk!" Monukuma was angry. Not only could he not land a hit on his former friend, but the slightly older man was also on him so quick that he wasn't able to get away. Jiro and Luna weren't fast enough, Ryo ended up closing the distance between him and Hanzo and landed a mighty blow to Hanzo's back. Hanzo staggered, but immediately caught his balance. When he was about to take care of Ryo, he froze almost as if he had seen a ghost.

"Ryoichi?" Hanzo said breathless, forgetting that he was in the middle of a battle. Ryo stopped then and stared at the man. For some odd reason, seeing the man up close made his head hurt. It was a pain that suggested that he was starting to remember something that he had forgotten. Almost in a trance, Ryo mumbled the words that Jiro wanted to confirm.

"Grandpa?" Ryo muttered, and Monukuma growled in anger. This was his chance! While Hanzo was distracted, Monukuma landed a powerful kick to Hanzo's arm, sending the old man flying across the room and smashing hard into the back wall.

"Ugh!" Hanzo groaned in pain.

"Grandpa!" Ryo shouted running over towards Hanzo.

"Hanzo!" Jiro and Luna followed.

"Tsk! I won't forget this. You ruined my plan and took one of my most cherished students. Ryo, since you will run and care for the enemy, you are nothing to me. You will pay, you will all pay!" With those parting words from Monukuma, he disappeared just before the police and EMS rushed into the building.

****

"I can't believe this," Ryoichi said as he sat outside Hanzo's hospital room. All this time he's been blindly following Monukuma-sensei listening to every word that he said about them changing the world for the better, seeing his grandfather's face for the first time in years, brought him back to reality. What Monukuma was doing was not bettering the world, it was terrorizing the world.

It sickened Ryoichi to know that he too, was brainwashed into terrorizing the world.

Jiro sat next to Ryoichi, whining a bit. Hanzo has never been hurt this badly before, so the fact that this had happened had Jiro feeling anxious. Ryoichi looked down at Jiro and patted his head.

"Words cannot describe how sorry I am for doing what I've done," Ryoichi said honestly. "Nothing can change what has happened, but at the very least I can help with finding the solution!" The Vice President announced a few hours ago that the President was wounded by a group of terrorists. It hurt Ryoichi to know that he was a part of the terrorist group.

"Ryoichi, it's alright. We will find the solution together," Jiro said. Ryo told Jiro everything that he knew. Ryo knew that Jiro would not be able to answer his questions with words, but Ryo knew that Jiro could understand him. The way that Jiro could fight like a confident human ninja, proved that Jiro could understand people.

Ryoichi told Jiro that the ninja organization ran by Monukuma was planning on eliminating the president, blame the act on another country, and amidst the confusion, they were meant to eliminate everyone who Monukuma deemed as a threat. This was an attempt to create a world where Monukuma and his ninja organization were the rulers.

Hanzo's books reveals the Hakumoto clan's techniques. Learning these techniques will give anyone the power to perform moves to take out hundreds of people at one time. The problem with the books was that it needed to be deciphered by a prophet for them to understand how to do the techniques. Jiro was glad that he and Luna had gotten to the ninjas before they made it to the prophet. Jiro was also thankful that Luna found Hanzo's books, which Monukuma left behind when he escaped. Jiro would have to thank Luna once he went back home.

"I've seen Monukuma brainwash many of our newer younger members. He has so many young ninjas because he believes that training them would be more beneficial than training older ones because of their agility and ability to learn quickly. However, I think he preys on young people because they will follow him blindly without asking questions. I can't believe that I was one of them." Ryo shook his head, and Jiro laid his paw on his leg. Jiro couldn't say anything that would comfort the young boy, but he at the very least could show him that he cared.

"We will do everything in our power to stop Monukuma and save all the children who were brainwashed. This is not your fault, you were a victim!" Jiro's words fell on deaf ears. Jiro and Luna managed to stop a tragedy from happening and saved Ryoichi; however, there was so much more that needed to be done.

Jiro was happy that he had found Hanzo's long lost grandson Ryoichi, but Jiro was upset that Hanzo couldn't enjoy the reunion yet. There was still so many things that needed to be done regarding Ryoichi. Naturally, Hanzo would want to get Ryoichi checked out by a doctor, but first Hanzo needed to get better.

The truth was finally revealed, but their journey was far from over. Things needed to be done, and questions still needed to be asked and answered. Exactly what has Hanzo been doing every day since the Hakumoto books were stolen? Why was Hanzo with the president? What was the deal between Hanzo and Monukuma? How was Monukuma able to brainwash so many people? Jiro needed to know these answers, but he needed everyone's help.

Soon the doctor exited the hospital room and told Ryoichi and Jiro that Hanzo would be okay and that he was sleeping. Jiro was thankful to hear that, but this wasn't the outcome that he had expected to happen. Though this wasn't a happy ending to the end of their day, it wasn't the true ending either. There was much to be done, and Jiro was going to make sure that he led Ryoichi down the right path from now on.

Jiro, Luna, Ryoichi, and Hanzo will reveal more truths soon, and put an end to Monukuma's devious ploy.

The End

CHARLIE
BOOK

17006660R00021

Made in the USA
Middletown, DE
27 November 2018